I love my granny

Giles Andreae & Emma Dodd

I love my granny. Can you tell?

She says I'm pretty great as well!

She's like a mum, but unlike mine,

she seems to have just loads of time.

I go round to her house to play,

And sometimes we just chat all day.

She knows a lot more things than me,

But then she's lived for ages, see?

She loves the photos Mummy sends,

And shows them off to all her friends.

She takes me out for special treats,

And sometimes buys us bags of sweets!

We ride on trains, and buses too,

and have adventures. Yes, we do!

We play all sorts of brilliant games,

And give each other silly names.

We really love to cook and bake,

And eat the yummy things we make.

We watch my favourites on TV,
And snuggle up, just her and me.
She's got a very comfy tummy.
"That," she says, "is very funny!"

And when it’s time to say goodbye,

My granny does a little sigh . . .

And says, although we've had such fun . . .

. . . it's nice to give me back to Mum.

I hope your granny's just like mine.

We really have the bestest time!